I0739216

Human Again

Nina Wirk

Human Again by Nina Wirk
Copyright © 2016 by Nina Wirk. All rights reserved.

This book or any portion thereof may not be reproduced or used in any manner whatsoever without the express written permission of the author except for the use of brief quotations in a book review.

This book is a work of fiction. Names, characters, businesses, places, events, and incidents are either the products of the author's imagination or used in a fictitious manner. Any resemblance to actual persons, living or dead, or actual events is purely coincidental.

Disclaimer: Although every precaution has been taken to verify the accuracy of the information contained herein, the author and publisher assume no responsibility for any errors or omissions. No liability is assumed for damages that may result from the use of information contained within.

Books are available from Amazon.com and other retail outlets.

Cover Painting by: Andrea Danti

Cover design by: Redbird Designs http://www.redbird-designs.net

Editing by:

1. Pink Flamingo Accurate Editing
http://pinkflamingoaccuratediting.weebly.com
Mandy Wirk, BSc, MA

2. Polgarus Studio
http://www.polgarusstudio.com

Library of Congress Control Number: 2016907352

LCCN Imprint Name: Nina Wirk

ISBN 13:   Print Book 978-0-9970431-4-3
             Kindle 978-0-9970431-5-0
             Epub 978-0-9970431-6-7

First Edition Printed in U.S.A.

*I dedicate this book to my biggest
cheerleaders:
thanks, Mom and Dad.*

"I think, therefore I am."

René Descartes

Contents

1
A Holiday

The fire alarm wailed. Still drunk with sleep, I raised my head from my pillow and gave a few owlish blinks to get my bearings. Rays of winter light poured through the cracks in the blinds and lit up the room. I hated Mondays, but this was a rare, precious day off to catch up on much-needed sleep and recuperate from the tribulations of the past week. I needed to recharge for the merciless onslaught of the workweek ahead. I shivered in the chilly room since I had been scrimping on the electricity bill by turning off the heat.

"Please go to the nearest exit without

delay. Do *not* take the elevator. Only use the stairs," the overhead speaker thundered in a shrill, robotic tone.

With any luck, it was a false alarm. But the incessant message blared every two minutes, alternating with the clanging fire alarm. It did not stop. The small one-bedroom apartment reverberated with the cacophony. Reaching for my cell phone on the nightstand, I checked the time. It was nine o'clock in the morning. The thought of getting dressed, descending eighteen flights of stairs, and trooping out of the apartment building to wait in the dank cold on the street outside in two feet of snow made me groan and cringe. Even though I pulled the blanket over my head and cocooned myself in its velvety warmth, hoping for a reprieve, there came a point when I could no longer ignore the caterwaul. My heart sank. What if this was a real fire? I kicked myself for not getting renter's insurance.

Visions of flames raging through the apartment spurred me to action. How could

I have been so nonchalant in the first place? I leaped out of bed, threw on an old sweater with elbow patches, and tucked my jeans into knee-high black leather boots. The buttons of my sweater were off kilter, but I didn't care. I pulled back my long black hair into a ponytail. Racing to the front door, I grabbed my coat and a bag containing my computer and essential documents that I had kept at the ready for a day like this. I fumbled with my keys and locked the front door. Dashing to the nearest exit just around the corner, I flew down the stairs. As I reached the bottom of the stairs, my heart was pounding. I flung open the door, stepped out onto the side street, and sprinted to the front of the apartment building. Relieved that I had made it out alive, I was shocked to find myself alone. Where on earth were the other tenants?

Through the falling snow, I recognized the haggard, emaciated homeless man in tatterdemalion clothes at his usual perch under the awning at the corner of the apartment building. He leaned against the wall, hung his head in despair, and studied the snow. Cars crawled with their headlights on, inching their way along the icy road. The sun was nowhere in sight on this gray, blustery day. A stout lady, who was swaddled in a duffle coat, tartan scarf, and earmuffs, stomped through the snow with her yellow Labrador Retriever on a leash. The puppy yelped and wagged its tail as it scurried to greet the homeless man. The itinerant soul glanced up for a brief moment, and a thin smile flickered on his craggy face as he stooped to pet the puppy.

"Now Susie, it's time to go home," the portly lady said in vexation.

She yanked the leash to coax the dog away but without success. So she scooped up the puppy and slogged through the snow. After she had swept past me and disappeared around the corner, I was left alone on the street. Even the homeless man had trudged away in search of shelter as the snow tumbled down with greater intensity. The snow muffled the roar of a lone snowplow rolling down the road. An eerie silence gripped the air. Why was I the only one hanging around here? Why had no fire engines arrived?

The wind howled a mournful dirge as it whistled in between the gleaming glass office towers and high-rise apartment buildings hugging both sides of the street. Snowflakes clung to my hair and eyelashes as in my haste I had forgotten to bring an umbrella. Unable to bear the biting cold any longer, I plodded through the snow to the leasing office that was at the corner of the building.

The teenage receptionist at the front desk put down her nail file as I entered and gave me a blank stare. She stopped chewing her gum for a brief moment. The corners of her mouth drooped in a scowl as if she resented this interruption.

"Hello, miss," she said. "May I help you? What apartment are you in?"

My teeth chattered as I spoke. "I'm in seven one four. Is the fire under control? Can we go back inside? Where are the fire engines? Are they around the back? Where is everybody?"

She scrunched her nose, furrowed her brow, and rolled her eyes. Her gruff tone jarred me at that early hour. "Didn't you get the notice we sent two weeks ago about the fire alarm test? There was no need to evacuate. We test the fire alarm at least once a year."

My exasperation bubbled to the surface. "I *never* received the notice. Isn't today January seventeenth? It's the Martin Luther King Day holiday. Why would you test the fire alarm *today* of all days?"

She flicked away the spiky bangs from her eyes. "We don't observe Martin Luther King Day. Many other businesses don't either. Besides, the fire alarm is only going to last for another twenty-five minutes. It'll be over with by ten o'clock."

Then she picked up her nail file and examined her hands, signaling that she wanted to get back to her nails. Taking the cue, I braced myself to go outside. The gusts of wind blew swirling eddies of snow in my face as I fought to reach the main entrance. The distance was only one hundred yards but seemed endless in the inclement weather. The snow crunched under my boots. Through the maelstrom of snow flurries, I could see the faint outline of the android guarding the entrance. After I had punched in an entry code in the security access panel on the wall, the android porter pried the door open against the force of the wind.

"Hello, Zena," the android said in a flat voice. "This snowstorm will last until dawn tomorrow, so it's best not to go outside."

I nodded in the affirmative. The android had an unlined face with vacant blue eyes that contrasted with its cadaverous complexion. Snow adhered to its blue jumpsuit, the standard android uniform. The first androids were manufactured in Silicon Valley thirty years ago. Now in 2180, androids had become ubiquitous all over the world. First, they had replaced humans as laborers in manufacturing, farms, and construction. Now they were taking over the service industry as well. I missed human waiters, hairdressers, and shop assistants—

they were extinct. Every so often, politicians would propose a universal basic income for humans to offset the scarcity of jobs, but it never materialized. In the end, no governmental agency could rustle up the money to fund such a proposal. It was the bleak era of scarcity and austerity everywhere in the world.

All androids looked alike because they were manufactured from the same template. At six feet four inches tall, androids towered over most humans. They had slim, androgynous bodies and faces with chiseled features. Even so, they communicated with the low-pitched voices of males. Their movements were graceful, making it difficult to distinguish them from humans at a distance. Up close, their deadpan facial expressions and taut, wrinkle-free, bloodless skin gave them away. Overall, they had cold-blooded demeanors and apathetic voices, regardless of the gravity of the situation. Even worse, their eyes were lifeless with fixed pupils.

After stamping my feet to get rid of the

snow, I entered. The menacing fire alarm still echoed through the building. I stopped in my tracks and shuddered upon glimpsing the ghostly, waif-like apparition in the ornate floor-to-ceiling mirror gracing the lobby. I peered into the mirror again. Was that really me? The dim lighting from the crystal chandelier hanging from the center of the cathedral ceiling seemed to accentuate my raccoon eyes. Without any under-eye concealer to hide the dark circles, I appeared dejected and haunted, like a lost kite scurrying about in shifting air currents, all the time preparing for a rough landing when the wind died. I tried to console myself with the thought that dark circles were a part of aging, although I was only thirty years old. No doubt, I could use more sleep, but that was easier said than done these days. Or, perhaps, the sense of impending doom from knowing my job as a bank teller was under threat from the androids not only paralyzed me with fear but also manifested on my face. I lived on borrowed time. Any day now, I could be out of work and join the faceless, nameless multitudes in the squatter camp on the outskirts of New York City. Was it our human destiny to be cast off to no-man's-land by the very society we helped to create?

2
Hope

I decided to snap out of my melancholy and do something useful by checking my car in the underground parking lot. Since the bank was only two blocks away, I walked to work every morning to stay fit. Besides, I would have to pay an extra one hundred dollars a month to park my vehicle at work, which I could ill afford in my current constrained circumstances. Why was everything in the city so expensive? So, to keep my car's battery from dying from a lack of use, I had to run the engine for about ten minutes once a week.

I lumbered down the stairs to the musty

subterranean garage. It was deserted save for a smattering of vehicles. Only the echoes of my footsteps pierced the stillness. I rubbed my hands together. It was even colder down in the garage than it was outside. As I approached my sturdy, ten-year-old Subaru Outback, I admired its sleek, aerodynamic teardrop shape. While revving up the engine, I realized that most people were at work, which was why the garage was so deserted, and why the apartment's management scheduled the fire alarm test today. They knew so few businesses observed Martin Luther King Day as a national holiday.

I wished I could have taken the elevator back up to my apartment, but the ongoing fire alarm forced me to climb nineteen flights of stairs. Near the top, I paused, holding onto the rail and gasping to catch my breath. I had not realized how deconditioned I was. I was panting by the time I arrived at my front door, and, as luck would have it, the alarm stopped just then.

Since the apartment was an icebox, I

turned the thermostat up a little. The wind rattled outside, so I rescued my sole plant, a Christmas cactus, from the balcony. Once inside, I dusted off the snow from the brilliant red flowers and displayed it on the coffee table, admiring how it added a splash of color to the otherwise drab décor. After changing back into my pajamas, I crawled into bed, hoping to nap for a few hours. Even so, the thought of going to work in the morning kept me awake. After an hour spent tossing and turning, I gave up on the idea of sleep and decided to browse through my favorite sites on the Internet instead.

I enjoyed catching up with my best friend Hope on her Facebook page. Hope lived on the seventh floor and worked in the bank as well. Her inspirational musings always bolstered my spirits. I smiled as I read Frances Hodgson Burnett's quote from *The Secret Garden*: "If you look the right way, you can see that the whole world is a garden." This posting was from two weeks ago, and there were no others, which was most unusual for her.

My mother's and grandmother's Facebook pages were also my favorite haunts. Although I had never met my grandmother, I had heard many stories about her exploits from my mother. For example, as the family's first member to get a college degree, Granny was a trailblazer. Moreover, I felt like I knew her from reading about her thoughts, feelings, milestones, likes, and dislikes. Today, I learned her favorite tea was Irish breakfast. In fact, Facebook had immortalized both Mom and Granny in virtual reality. For the past year, since my mother's death, I had been paying a daily pilgrimage to her Facebook page because it helped me to cope with the loss. As I thought about my Facebook page after my death, I trembled, wondering who would visit my virtual graveyard.

I was a foster child, raised by a single mother in Providence, Rhode Island. Although I never knew my biological parents, I was lucky to find such a loving and caring foster mother. During my rebellious teenage years, I often questioned my purpose in life. In the end, my foster mother revealed to me that I had been abandoned as a baby in the bushes on a street outside an android manufacturing plant in Providence. As fate would have it, she happened to be walking by and heard my mournful cries. On rescuing me, she decided to adopt me, for she said I was a "miracle baby who would do something important one day." Throughout her life, she held firm to her belief that even the smallest acts of kindness and generosity by the least of us can cause a ripple effect to change the world. Over the years, as I slipped into the anonymity of life in New York City's concrete jungle, it became more and more implausible that I would do something important. I was also beginning to lose faith that kindness mattered in such a cold world where only profit margins reigned supreme.

A rat-a-tat at the door roused me. I jolted up from the bed and threw on my dressing gown. Through the peephole, I saw Hope.

"I'm so glad you came," I said.

Hope hurried inside. Her ill-fitting gray tracksuit hung about her lanky, skin-and-bones frame, making her appear even gaunter. She was out of breath, for she had followed her usual practice of eschewing the elevator in favor of climbing the eighteen flights of stairs from the first-floor gym.

"I should also go to the gym," I said as I closed the door behind her. "Somehow, I never find the time. What a fright I had this morning with the alarm. Did you get the notice for the fire alarm testing?"

Hope nodded her head and collapsed onto the sofa. Her green eyes contrasted with her ebony complexion. She kept her curly black hair in a chignon at the nape of her neck. Her slender shoulders slumped, and her head drooped as she studied the oak laminate floor.

I flopped into the armchair opposite her. "Would you like some tea? Oh my, it's already lunchtime. Where did the time go? I made some chicken curry and basmati rice yesterday from my mom's favorite recipe.

She called it the Patel family's secret recipe."

Hope looked up. "I could use some tea and sympathy, Zena."

I sprang up from the armchair, and in three strides, I was in the kitchen. Only a small circular oak dining table separated the kitchen from the living room, so I carried on chatting with Hope as I prepared the tea and warmed the leftover chicken curry. "I noticed you haven't posted anything on Facebook for the past few weeks. Your inspirational quotes always give me a boost. Has something happened?"

Hope rubbed her eyes and massaged her temples. She spoke in a woebegone voice. "Nothing has happened. That's the problem. The sameness of the lackluster days bites the most. One banal day rolls into the next, and I carry on eking out a meager living to pay my bills. Is that all life is: working to pay off bills and then dying? I pray for something great to happen that would change my life for the better, but I'm still waiting. I am a number. I don't even feel human anymore."

"I know what you mean," I said.

"I'm tired of this rat race," Hope said. "I don't mind being a bank teller, but I can't stand our bank manager. He's such a crotchety old man who badgers me about my efficiency. Every week, he tells me I should be faster because my customer queues are too long. He fails to understand some transactions can't be hurried. How much harder can we work? He has already shortened our lunch hour to fifteen minutes and done away with our coffee breaks. Worse still, we're being forced to paste a fake smile on our faces all day long. I've even forgotten how to smile. I've never had the courage to complain about our unreasonable working conditions because I'm terrified of losing my job to the androids."

I placed the tea tray on the coffee table, along with plates of chicken curry, fluffy basmati rice, and chewy chocolate chip cookies.

After sipping some tea, Hope continued. "I wish I could study architecture at university, but there's no hope of that. It's too expensive. How can I save up for university when all my money goes to paying rent? Just like a rat scampering on a pet wheel in a cage, my life is going nowhere. With each passing year, I'm afraid I'll just accept my cage and that any chance or hope of doing great things will vanish forever."

Hope's words tugged at my sensibilities. I tried putting up a brave front. "I understand. Sometimes, I feel as if I'm on an out-of-control high-speed train going nowhere, without any station stops. Still, I believe change is the one constant in the universe. Change will come in its own time. No situation is permanent."

Even though I said that to reassure Hope, I was also trying to convince myself. In many ways, I was quickly losing confidence that I would ever be able to get out of the sinkhole threatening to engulf me.

Hope grimaced and wrung her hands. "There's something else. I realized if I was in trouble, there would be no one I could call for help. My parents and sister are so far away in Nigeria. Sometimes I want to go back to Nigeria as well. I remember our weekly feast days where we shared an evening meal together with all the residents of our neighborhood. It was a block party of sorts. I had such a happy childhood! I grew up with friends all around me. Here, in this entire twenty-story apartment building, you're my only friend."

I felt somewhat crestfallen. "You know you can always call me if you're in trouble. Always—I mean that. They say the luckiest people are the ones with happy childhoods. I had a happy childhood too. At least, we can hold on to those wonderful memories."

After a few bites of the spicy chicken curry and a few swigs of the aromatic Earl Grey tea, Hope relaxed back into the sofa and propped up her feet on the ottoman. "I know you're my best friend, but what I'm referring to is when the androids take my job away from me. What will I do, then? I've never trained for anything else. These days, your job defines your position in society.

Without a job, I'll be a nobody. I'll have to join the ranks of the forgotten homeless on the fringes of the city."

"The bank management hasn't said anything yet about replacing us with androids," I said. "Let's find out if anything has changed. There's usually an announcement about job closures at the end of the news."

I put on the television. A hologram of the android news anchor appeared in the corner of living room. "A very warm welcome to our worldwide audience. Thank you for joining us. Topping our news today is the ongoing fighting in the one hundred and seventy-seven-year war in the Middle East. The android army of the Western coalition has made substantial gains in Iraq, forcing the enemy android battalion to retreat. The superior drone airpower of the Western forces played a significant role in the latest push to regain lost territory. Let's go live now to the front line where our reporter is interviewing General Clyde Jacobs-Marsh."

A hologram materialized of another

android and a man in khaki battle fatigues and a green beret. They stood on a cliff overlooking a desert valley in which the two opposing android armies in head-to-toe titanium armor faced each other off, ready for combat. Drones circled overhead like eagle-eyed predators waiting for their prey. Monolithic army tanks rolled into position in between the two armies.

"General Jacobs-Marsh, when do you foresee an end to the war that began in 2003?" the android asked.

The brawny general's wrinkled face came into focus. He squinted in the blazing sun, puffed out his beefy barrel chest, and lifted up his double chin. His piano-key smile exuded confidence as he grandstanded for the audience. "That's not for me to say. I take my marching orders from Washington. What I can attest to is that we're bringing the insurgency to heel at a faster pace than ever before. The insurgents can replace any loss of their soldiers in a matter of days with a three-dimensional printer. It only takes three days to make another android. Our side, of course, has superior manufacturing capabilities."

As the general turned around and pointed to the flat-floored valley below, the impressive row of medals over the left breast pocket of his uniform glinted in the sun. "You can see our forces are three times larger than our enemy's, which gives us an edge in this conflict. I'm certain the humans who are now in refugee camps in neighboring countries will be able to return to their homes very soon."

"Thanks, General Jacobs-Marsh," the pallid android said in a monotone. "Now back to the main studio in New York."

"I liked human reporters so much more," I said.

Hope cast her tired eyes in my direction. "Why? Human reporters showboated for the cameras and lobbed the same softball questions as the androids do now. They're cut from the same cloth. I wish we had a way of learning what's really happening. I've always wondered what the government's real agenda is."

In the studio, the android news anchor sat next to a bland, bald man who had a circular face and rotund habitus. The man wore black Wayfarer glasses and a nondescript gray suit. In fact, everything about this human blob was gray, even his skin.

First, the android reeled off the humdrum business news, dealing with company mergers, the creation of megalithic conglomerates, and skyrocketing financial profits for the powerful elite.

Then the android turned toward the gray man. "We are lucky to have Donegal Cairn with us today from Hundun Corporation, the largest defense contractor in the world. Mr. Cairn, you heard the interview with General Jacobs-Marsh. How have you been shoring up the country's defenses?"

Donegal Cairn spoke in a dreary drone, much like the androids. "Since the start of the Iraq war, Hundun Corporation has supplied androids, tanks, and weapons to the Western coalition. This week, we received another government contract to build eight new manufacturing plants in

America and Iraq. Our goal is full production capacity within six months. With the war spreading to neighboring countries in the Middle East, the demand for weapons has become even more urgent. We have also developed technology to shorten the construction time on android soldiers from three days to two days, giving us a significant advantage on the battlefield. Although the production is mechanized, we'll be hiring sixteen human employees to manage the new munitions factories."

"I see that your company's share prices are skyrocketing on the stock market with these new contracts," the android said. "Thank you, Mr. Cairn, for your update. In our final few minutes of the show, let's recap the latest job layoffs. Last week, androids replaced grocery store clerks, and now doctors across all specialties will be phased out. The first hospitals to be affected will be in New York City; however, over the course of the next six months, this will spread worldwide. An oversight committee of five human doctors in each hospital will remain to ensure a smooth transition. That's all from Planetary News. We will leave you with a concert at the Lincoln Memorial in commemoration of Martin Luther King Day."

As the stirring "We Shall Overcome" music from the Washington Philharmonic Orchestra filled the tiny apartment, Hope perked up for a moment, but then her gloom deepened. "Zena, although we're safe for now, it's only a matter of time before they ax us too. If human doctors are expendable, so are bank tellers. It seems Martin Luther King's dream of equality, justice, and freedom remains only a dream after all these years."

"At least we have jobs even if it's for the short-term," I said.

The piquant, fulsome flavor of the chicken curry had done much to revive my flagging spirits and brighten my outlook somewhat. I dunked a chocolate chip cookie into the tea and savored the comforting treat, thankful for the reprieve, no matter how brief. I stretched back in my chair to enjoy the world's foremost soprano singing "We Shall Overcome." Tameka Williams was a human. No android could replicate her sublime, lilting vocal tones: at least not yet. Androids had taken over most human jobs, but they had yet to match human creativity in fields such as music, art, literature, research, and innovation. I took some solace in knowing the best inventors were still human.

When the heart-wrenching ode to human rights and justice was over, I closed my eyes with dread. "The thought of going to work tomorrow gives me the creeps. The bank manager wants to see me first thing in the morning. What could the meeting be about?"

Hope furrowed her forehead, ran her fingers through her hair, and darted her eyes around the room. She spoke with a quavering voice. "I got the same notice. I thought it might relate to a customer complaint about the long wait times at my kiosk. God knows, I work as fast as I can, but it's never good enough for them. Zena, since we're going to the same meeting, it has to be something else. There was no mention of replacing bank tellers with androids, so we must be safe. What do you think?"

I shrugged and turned the television off. Hope helped me to clear the lunch away. Her eyes were downcast. Only the clatter of the dishes, pots, and pans punctuated the solemn silence.

"Look Hope, no matter what happens tomorrow, remember we're in this together," I said. "You're not alone."

Hope managed a tight-lipped smile. Her upper lip quivered, though. "You're the best friend ever, Zena. I bet it's a meeting about an obscure procedure at the bank that we should follow. I'd better go. Thanks for the delicious lunch. I feel much better now. See you tomorrow."

However, she looked even sadder than when she had arrived. She wrapped her arms around herself and trudged out. Although I tried to lose myself in the mundaneness of cleaning the apartment, doing laundry, and paying overdue bills, I still fretted about the meeting in the morning. Not even a delicious supper of homemade lasagna could cheer me up. I kept wondering if the ax would fall tomorrow.

3
The Spark

As soon as my head touched the memory foam pillow, I dozed off, only to awake moments later in fright, gasping for air and sweating. Starlight bathed the room. On occasion, the frantic sound of ambulance sirens pierced the gloom. The impending meeting with the bank manager filled my being with dread. After realizing it was still the midnight hour, I breathed a sigh of relief.

I stared out of the large window at the starry night, ruminating on every possible outcome of the meeting in the morning. To escape my fear, I imagined Earth in the infinity of the universe. I lived on a pale blue dot in an anonymous corner of the cosmos that no extraterrestrial life had bothered to visit. Surely, my problems could not be so important as to paralyze me with fear. All of a sudden, the massive black hole in the center of the Milky Way galaxy swallowed me from which I had no way out. In a fit of despair, I held my head in my hands and mouthed a silent scream like Edvard Munch's painting, *The Scream.*

All too soon, the starlight gave way to the first ashen rays of the sun at five o'clock in the morning. The day had yet to begin, but I was already exhausted. My stomach churned as I thought of going to work. After a hurried cup of tea, I mustered up my waning energy and put on my uniform: a crisp white shirt and a black pantsuit. Only layers of pancake makeup could mask my raccoon eyes. After putting on my boots, coat, and green plaid scarf, I dashed out the door with my computer bag. Soon, the elevator's claustrophobic silence engulfed me as it *whished* down to the ground floor.

A bleary-eyed Hope was already pacing the lobby. Her contorted, wan face had a pained expression. She attempted a half-hearted smile. "I'm glad we're going together. I can use some moral support."

"Me too," I replied.

She smacked her lips together. "My mouth feels so dry, even though I drank five cups of water this morning."

The android porter stood outside, oblivious to the pelting rain, and held the door open. "Have a good day, ladies."

The rain battered the snow, thunder growled, and a lightning bolt set the morning sky aglow. The sun hid behind the nimbostratus clouds, the color of coal tar. A gale force wind from the Atlantic Ocean shrieked like a bat out of hell. Moreover, the ill wind thrashed the rain at an almost horizontal angle, collapsing our umbrellas and rendering them useless. I pulled down the hood of my coat.

Cars paraded along the street with their fog lights ablaze. Impatient drivers honked their horns. A sky train swooshed by overhead. On the left, I glimpsed the homeless man, slouching against the wall in his customary position at the corner of the apartment building. We made a right turn and slogged through the slush, past the hologram television shop and the grocery store, to reach a hundred-story glass building: the Ten Nations Bank. From a distance, it resembled a golden needle poking the sky. The ground floor was the community bank, and the upper floors housed the worldwide headquarters of the financial behemoth.

The automatic glass door slid open, and we trudged past a row of four abstract sculptures and the bank tellers' booths. The clacking of our boots on the marble floor echoed in the cavernous lobby. Rain droplets fell from our coats, leaving a trail of puddles across the marble floor. All the sculptures were computer generated except for my favorite one at the end: *The Galaxy of Stars* by Aldous Worthington. Although the spiral contours and twinkling lights of *The Galaxy of Stars* sculpture always managed to cheer me up, today tears welled up in my eyes. I longed for space travel to be available to the public. I would be the first in line to purchase a one-way ticket into the heavens, far away from the quagmire on Earth.

No one else had arrived yet. It was only ten minutes to seven, and we were early. The meeting was in an aseptic conference room next to the row of bank tellers' booths. As we entered, a homunculus's head popped up from behind a lectern at the front of the room. It was Norbert Linge, the bank manager.

He waved, and for the first time in recent memory, he greeted us with an ear-to-ear smile. "Hello, ladies. Have a seat. There's a coat rack at the back. The meeting starts at seven o'clock sharp."

Norbert Linge had patchy white hair and an equally sparse Salvador Dali white mustache and goatee. He had a peculiar habit of spitting out his words, so it was best to maintain a safe distance from him. As we settled in the middle of the room, choosing to keep our coats on in case of the need for a fast getaway, he glared at us with his beady, saurian eyes that cast a chill in the air.

The conference room had a seating capacity of twenty. There were ten rectangular cardboard boxes on a table by the lectern. A colossal computer-generated painting dominated the right wall. Every time I viewed the intricate series of interconnecting cogs, psychedelic colors, and harsh edges, I heard clicking and grinding noises, and today was no exception. My temples throbbed with pain, and waves of nausea wracked my body. The message was loud and clear; I was a minor cog in a machine.

In a piecemeal fashion, the remaining eight bank tellers shuffled in and huddled together at the back of the room. The bank tellers hailed from countries all over the world: India, China, Burma, Japan, Bolivia, Jamaica, and Mexico, among others. They had saturnine countenances and doleful eyes as if they expected the worse. I had toiled alongside them for over ten years, but the days were so hectic that we remained just passing acquaintances.

Meanwhile, the bank manager strutted around the room and glanced at his watch with impatience. His wrathful glances ricocheted around the room. Just then, the assistant bank manager, Robert Brown-Lee traipsed in five minutes late and plopped into a chair next to the lectern. He was a bald, short man with an impish grin and a protruding belly, which forced him to leave his gunnery-green tweed jacket open.

"Welcome, ladies," the bank manager said with a hint of Schadenfreude in his cheery voice. "I'm glad you made it in the rainstorm. Let's get right down to business. As you know, we've had a litany of complaints from irate customers about the slow service you provide. Nobody has escaped criticism. Customers are deserting us for other banks, and our share price is plummeting. 'Efficient service' is the motto of the Ten Nations Bank. To compete on the cutthroat world stage, we have to increase our efficiency. So, we have no choice but to innovate. To that end, we're spearheading a new initiative to become the first bank in the world to switch to android bank tellers."

He paused and pranced down the central aisle like a coxcomb, peering at each of us in turn with glee. The collective grief among us crescendoed and permeated the room like a thick, impervious fog. Hope wiped away the tears rolling down her cheeks. I remained stoic only because I felt numb after staying up all night.

With an air of satisfaction, Norbert Linge stood at the front of the room with his legs akimbo. His face cracked into a Cheshire cat smile. "Embrace the day, ladies, for a new day has dawned for each of you. You are young. The young always think they can make a difference. You will receive two weeks of severance pay. Unemployment insurance, at forty percent of your present salary, will kick in today as well and continue for four months, giving you enough time to plan your next step. It's a generous offer. Other institutions would not be half as accommodating. Mr. Brown-Lee, the assistant bank manager, will oversee the android bank tellers. Mr. Brown-Lee do you have anything to add?"

The assistant bank manager held onto the chair as he rose to face us. With his other hand, he wiped his red button nose. Then he flashed a cheesy grin and spoke in a sheepish tone. "You've been most thorough, Mr. Linge. The androids are hard at work as we speak. It's quite extraordinary. Automation is a wonderful thing. Customers are happier since they no longer have to wait in line. The androids will vault us to the top of the stock market."

Norbert Linge's smile widened. He pointed to the brown boxes on the table. "Ah, that's music to my ears: efficiency on a grand scale. Ladies, we cleared out your lockers, and the contents are in these boxes with your names on them. Before you claim your box, hand in your identification badges and keys. Mr. Brown-Lee will sign you out. Make sure you exit by the front door without disturbing any of the customers. Don't dawdle."

He clapped to hurry us along and then sashayed out the room. As the sounds of his cackling laughter receded, a desultory queue formed in the aisle. I handed over my keys and badge to Mr. Brown-Lee and scribbled my signature on the dotted line. After collecting my box, I lingered at the back of the room, waiting for Hope.

"Well, that's over with," I said as she approached.

"Linge and Brown-Lee could have included a few words of thanks for our hard work," Hope said. "It's as if all those years of toil meant nothing. They think humans are disposable now that androids can work twenty-four seven without bathroom breaks. I guess not having to pay the androids any wages or benefits, like health insurance or sick leave, will also help the bank's bottom line. The androids have taken over the workplace. Whatever happened to the human touch?"

I opened the door. "Let's get out of here."

The bank was a beehive of activity. The androids had settled into our former booths as if they had worked there forever. They beavered away and set a dizzying pace. Mr. Brown-Lee was right; the habitual long queues that formed at this hour had vanished. I doubted that any of the customers even noticed our absence. I knew I was an unwelcome stranger who could never belong in this space. We shambled past the abstract sculptures in silence and spilled out onto the street that was bustling with people and cars. A contingent of androids marched by us with their eyes peeled ahead. It seemed life carried on, without missing a heartbeat.

Even though in one fell swoop I had lost my job and my place in society, I felt liberated, strange to say. My worst fears had materialized, but I was still alive. The rain had petered down to a light drizzle. Up above, the sun peeked through the coal-tar clouds. I gulped lungfuls of air. Without a word, the other sacked bank tellers went their separate ways, like flimsy boats adrift in a storm.

"Hope, can we go to the grocery store?" I

said. "It's on our way home. I ran out of milk. There's a coffee shop in the grocery store. I could use a cup of coffee. Look, we have four months to figure things out. This wasn't that great of a job."

Hope gulped back her tears. "What a snake-bitten day. I won't miss the job. Who could miss the bank manager? It's the way they treated us—as if we were expendable nobodies. It's a merciless world, Zena, with no sense of human decency. What's the value of a human these days? With androids taking over human jobs, what are we meant to do? Jobs for humans are becoming nonexistent. The maintenance and repair of androids were once the only secure jobs for people. Now even that's done by other androids. Only human artists, musicians, and inventors are still in demand, but for how much longer? I was never that good at arts or science. I'm going back to Nigeria. I miss my family. I feel better already now that I've decided. Yes, let's go to the grocery store. I need a few things too."

"I wish you wouldn't go back to Nigeria,

but I understand," I said.

We navigated through the throng and reached the grocery store in the next block. An android porter patrolled the entrance of the two-story building. A blue-and-green neon sign flashed "Fresh Food Marketplace." We placed our boxes in the shopping carts and rolled them inside. A bevy of shoppers hummed around the store. Android grocery store clerks wheeled crates on trolleys in the produce section, culling any fruit and vegetables with blemishes or those nearing the expiration date. These they discarded in large bins at the back of the grocery store.

"It seems a shame so much food goes to waste," I said. "They're throwing away good food on the day before its expiration date."

"I read somewhere up to forty percent of the food is thrown out," Hope said in a bleak voice. "And people are going hungry because they can't afford the exorbitant prices of food. Well, what can we do about it?"

"Do you think humans have a shelf-life

too?" I said. "Are we getting close to our expiration dates and becoming obsolete?"

In a pensive mood, Hope walked on without replying. By that time, we had reached the dairy aisle. Right away, I recognized the homeless man who always stood outside the apartment building. A putrid smell, like rotting fish, wafted out from his person. Sooty grime clung to his face, and a tangled mop of gray hair fell to his shoulders. He tied his black plastic raincoat with a frayed string. His big toes peeped out of his shoes, and his trousers had patches here and there. After snatching a carton of milk from the shelf, he scurried off, without a word.

Before long, Hope and I waited in the express checkout line. Ahead of us was an impatient businessman who kept glancing at his watch and tapping his fingers on the edge of the conveyor belt. At the front of the line, the homeless man was emptying his basket on the conveyer belt: milk, apples, and oatmeal cookies. The cash register jingled as the android grocery store clerk tallied the sundry items and packed them in a paper bag with the store's logo: a sunflower.

"Eight dollars and fifty-two cents," the android said.

"I have a dollar I can give you," the homeless man replied in a hoarse voice. "I'm so hungry and thirsty. I haven't had any food for days. Can you make an exception? It won't happen again; I promise you."

The businessman picked up a tabloid newspaper from the checkout lane magazine rack and began thumbing through it as if he had not heard the desperate plea.

"I will call the store manager," the android said.

The cash register was open, and the android's arm rested on the till. Just as the android was about to press the button for the manager, it froze. Instead, the android studied the floor as if it was searching a memory bank for what to do next.

"I'll help," I said. "I can pay."

All at once, the android lifted its head up and stared at me. I had the fleeting impression that a spark had ignited in its once vacuous blue eyes.

"You will pay, and he is hungry," the android said. "You will pay, and he is hungry. You will help."

The homeless man turned around and peered at me through the shaggy fringe covering his eyes. "Thanks."

"Yes, here's the money," I said to the android.

The android shook its head. "There is no need to pay. He is hungry. He needs food. He has not eaten for days."

Hope whispered in my ear. "What do you think is happening? This android doesn't seem like any of the others. Has it malfunctioned?"

In a flash, the homeless man scooped up his goods and staggered only a few paces before he collapsed on the floor and knelt as if he was about to pray. Instead, he rummaged through his bag for the milk carton and tore it open with shaking hands. He lifted the carton to his lips, tilted his head back, and guzzled half its contents in one go.

His gulps echoed in my ears. A stream of milk flowed from the corner of his mouth. He wiped it away and licked his hand, not wanting to waste a single precious drop. Oblivious to the gawking passersby, he squeezed his eyes shut and bowed his head, relishing the nutrition flowing through his veins.

Meanwhile, the businessman placed a six-pack of beer on the conveyer belt.

"Three dollars please," the android said.

"I hadn't realized the beer was on sale, or I would have picked up another," the businessman said, grinning.

After paying, he sidestepped the homeless man, who was still kneeling on the floor, and made a hasty exit. The other checkout stands were buzzing as well. Customers bubbled with excitement as they spoke with the androids. As I emptied my basket and placed the milk and shortbread cookies on the conveyer belt, I studied the android again. The spark in its blue eyes persisted. A broad, hearty smile had replaced its mirthless demeanor. Instead of a monotone voice, the android's speech matched the cadences and inflection of a human.

"Four dollars and twelve cents," the android said.

"Are you sure?" I asked. "The price for these items is listed as twelve dollars."

"Yes, I am certain," the android said. "The actual price is four dollars and twelve cents, according to the cost of production and transportation."

While I paid, the store manager, a human, arrived in a frenzied state. He had a ballooning waistline and a gap between his two front teeth. He frowned and adopted a pugilistic mien as he spoke in a voice like a booming foghorn. He wagged his finger at the android. "I've been watching you. Why did you let that homeless man go without paying? You're more or less giving the paying customers fifty percent off. Do you think we're running a charity? This is a business."

The unfazed android looked at him with benevolent eyes. "Sir, the man had not eaten for days. I analyzed all the historical texts in the world on the right course of action. There was only one possible solution: to allow him to eat because he was hungry. As to these prices, I have tabulated the costs of the entire world's food supply from production to transportation, and this is the actual price of the food. You are overcharging the customers."

The store manager clasped the android's arm and shook it. "What's wrong with you? You've malfunctioned, and now your disease is spreading to the other androids like an out of control contagion. This store has gone to hell. Where are those androids going?"

Instead of throwing away the food items that were nearing expiration, the androids wheeled the trolleys to the street and left the crates there for passersby to sample. Through the glass door, I glimpsed the homeless man among the gaggle of pedestrians who swarmed around the crates of food. He filled his bag with fruit and vegetables and gobbled down two muffins with glee. For the first time in a long while, I saw Hope's face wreathed in smiles. I laughed too. The world seemed a little bit brighter to me all of a sudden.

"I'll shut all of you down," the store manager said, pointing an accusatory finger at the row of android grocery store clerks. "Just you wait till the central office hears about this."

He whipped out his cell phone and explained the situation to the store's headquarters. "What do you mean? Why can't you shut off these scumbags? What am I supposed to do? All right then, I'll wait until you contact the Advanced Thinking Technology Company that manufactured these cretin androids. In the meantime, I'll call the police to have these rejects removed."

In less than a minute, police sirens blared outside. As soon as the two police androids marched inside, the store manager waved them down.

"Oh, thanks for coming," he said. "I'm at my wits' end. These androids are all out of control. They're giving the food away. Can you remove these losers?"

The two police androids frowned. Androids never frown. They were programmed to have no facial expressions. I was startled. What was happening? They had the same spark in their eyes as the grocery store android. It was as if the androids had come alive. But how could that be? Without even talking to the grocery store clerk, the police androids had ascertained what had transpired with the homeless man. Was there telepathy between the androids?

"No one has committed a crime," the police android said. "The android grocery store clerk gave a hungry man food to eat. Since you are overcharging the customers, the price for the food must be cut."

The store manager held his head in his hands and lamented. "I give up. I give up."

Seething with rage, he clenched his teeth and fists as he backed away from the checkout stand in a daze. Then, he whirled around, sprinted to his office at the front of the grocery store, slammed the door shut, and locked himself inside. Meanwhile, hordes of people were pouring into the grocery store. Word had traveled fast about the store's largesse. The two police androids stood sentry in a corner and surveyed the crowd.

While waiting for Hope, I strolled to the adjoining checkout stand. Indeed, a spark had ignited in that android's eyes as well. The human customers fizzed with exuberance, like a newly opened bottle of champagne.

As soon as Hope joined me, we cleaved a path through the teeming clamor. The long line of eager customers in the packed coffee shop at the front of the store deterred us from venturing there to have a cup of coffee. An even larger crowd was milling around outside the store, rummaging through the crates of food. A television crew pulled up to the Fresh Food Marketplace and unloaded a slew of camera equipment. For some inexplicable reason, the crew was all human in place of the customary androids.

Hope and I sallied forth, past the vacant building next to the grocery store. A jubilant throng that had congregated outside the hologram television store hampered our progress, so we decided to join them.

I pointed to the shop window where a hologram television was projecting the latest news. "Oh, *wow!* I can't believe it. The homeless from the shantytown in no-man's-land have broken through the razor wire fences and are heading for the grocery stores. What happened here is spreading to all the grocery stores in the city."

A hologram of an android news reporter appeared. "Thanks for joining us for this breaking news. We have the pleasure of interviewing Kenneth Puddingstone, the chief executive officer of the Fresh Food Marketplace conglomerate. Sir, tell us more about what happened today in your grocery stores throughout the country."

Kenneth Puddingstone had a peeved expression on his face. He crinkled his aquiline nose and scowled. "An egregious mistake has happened, but we hope to correct it very soon and get back to the way things were. The androids in our grocery stores have malfunctioned and are giving away food to the homeless and destitute. They claim we are overcharging our customers, but that's a downright lie. We have always been fair and equitable. We should never have transitioned to android grocery store clerks. At least, our human employees followed the rules to the letter."

The android reporter referred to a screen showing the actual and listed price of common household items. "Sir, how do you answer to these price differences? You are price-gouging by charging twice as much. In most languages, that is called greed."

Kenneth Puddingstone turned crimson and stared openmouthed at the android reporter. He wiped off rivulets of sweat from his forehead with a handkerchief from his lapel pocket and twisted his lips into a carnivorous smirk. "How dare you insinuate..."

Out of the blue, the hologram vanished. Someone had canned the show. Thunderous applause erupted in the slack-jawed audience outside the shop window. Fearless cries of "truth and justice" and "greedy crooks" rippled like waves through the crowd.

"The androids are linked," Hope said. "Androids were manufactured from a single template at the Advanced Thinking Technology Company. If the androids in this country are functioning as one, then it's only a matter of time before this phenomenon spreads to the rest of the world."

I beamed from ear to ear. "This morning, I cursed my fate. I thought my life was over. Now it's turning out to be a dazzling new day."

The crowd began to disperse. Next to the hologram television shop was an abandoned business with shuttered and boarded windows. As a group of five androids approached us, they nodded and smiled. It seemed like quite an innocuous thing to do, except that androids usually marched by with their gazes fixed straight ahead. As soon as they arrived at the building, they opened their toolboxes and proceeded to remove the shutters and boards in an efficient manner.

"Hello," I said. "This building has been vacant for as long as I can remember."

When the android swiveled around, its eyes shone with understanding and depth. "We are refurbishing abandoned buildings to provide free housing for the poor and homeless. Vacant homes in this country outnumber the homeless six to one. There are seventy-seven thousand abandoned government buildings as well that we can use."

The androids resumed their task with vigor. I was flabbergasted.

"What a brilliant idea to solve the housing crisis for the homeless," Hope said, smiling.

"Let's celebrate today," I said. "Want to have some lunch? I have homemade lasagna sitting in my fridge."

We rushed home in high spirits. The surly teenage receptionist greeted us at the door in place of the android porter. She held the door open and sneered. "We've removed all the androids from our premises until we can determine why they're malfunctioning."

Upon returning to my apartment, Hope flopped into the sofa, and a shadow came over her. "They'll probably find a way to reprogram the androids back to the way they were. Nothing good ever lasts."

I warmed up the leftover lasagna. "How can we ever return to the way things were? It would be intolerable. Maybe there'll be more information on the news."

Hope turned on the television. The broadcast from Iraq showed an android reporter interviewing General Jacobs-Marsh. In the valley below, the android troops had disbanded, and the tanks were rolling away. Without a mighty army to command, the general looked like a chest-thumping hero of a B-movie.

"To our viewers around the world, thank you for joining us for this breaking news," the android said. "We are live on the front line of the war in Iraq. General Jacobs-Marsh is the war over?"

The general fumed and bellowed. "How

can the war be over? The android soldiers are cowards. They've run away from the battlefield in the thick of war with their tails between their legs. We'll decommission them and build new ones."

"General Jacobs-Marsh, the war has lasted a hundred and seventy-seven years," the android replied. "Maybe they are tired of fighting. What is the purpose of war? Are there any winners in a war?"

The unexpected questions unhinged General Jacobs-Marsh. The veins in his neck became engorged with blood as if he was about to explode. "You're another one of these sissy android pacifists. I refuse to carry on an interview with a malfunctioning android."

He stomped off in a huff. Next, the broadcast shifted to the studio in New York City where a human reporter was anchoring the news. He flashed a gummy smile, but he could not hide the panic in his eyes. "As you've seen, the android armies in Iraq have packed up and gone. We still don't know whether our government will declare peace.

However, androids fighting wars all around the world have likewise deserted the battlefields. For the first time in history, there is no war anywhere on the planet. From Sudan to the South China Sea Islands, the guns and bombs are silent. The android revolution has filled the silence."

I stopped eating the scrumptious lasagna. The images of all the empty battlefields in the world astounded me. Hope held her hand over her mouth and gazed with wide-eyed wonder at the astonishing scenes.

"I never thought I would live to see a day without a war raging somewhere in the world," I said. "Things are moving fast. These androids have put humans to shame. What a miserable world humans have created where all we do is eke out a living, pay our bills, and fight endless battles. Speaking of money, I wonder if the bank manager made good on his word and deposited two weeks' salary into our accounts. My rent check is due soon."

I searched for my bank account on my cell phone. I had no confidence in the bank manager's word, so when a million-dollar balance popped up in my account, my heart skipped a beat, and I almost choked. I was dumbfounded.

Hope fumbled in her bag for her cell phone to check her own account. "What's wrong, Zena? Did that scoundrel Linge renege on his word? *Wowee*! My bank balance is a million dollars. Did those new android bank tellers make a mistake?"

I curled up on the armchair. "Mine is a million dollars too. This is manna from heaven. I've lived from month to month with seldom more than two thousand dollars in my account. I was so worried last night that I didn't even sleep. I thought the world had ended, but today is the best day ever. What a great start to 2180: an annus mirabilis. Are we going to wake up and find this is only a dream?"

Hope pinched herself. "No, this isn't a dream. It's for real. I wonder how my mom's doing in Nigeria. I'll find out if the android revolution has spread to Nigeria."

Before she had the chance to phone, a series of ominous thumps at the door awoke us from our blissful reverie. Still giddy with joy, I opened the door. Five policemen prowled around the hallway. They carried batons and laser guns. I was puzzled at seeing human policemen because androids had filled that role for the past year.

A burly policeman stepped forward. His thin lips twitched, and his eyes hardened. "Are you Zena Patel? Is Hope Adeola here? Both of you are to come with us to the station."

My heart quaked. I marshaled my thoughts, but I could only stammer. "Um, why? We haven't done anything wrong."

Hope turned off the television and staggered to the door. "There must be some mistake."

As if by instinct, the policeman fingered his gun in his belt holster. He bared his teeth and spat his words in a menacing tone. "No miss, there's no mistake. You're to come for an interview. If you don't make any trouble, this will soon be over."

We grabbed our coats and purses. The policemen encircled us and steered us to the elevator.

4
Revolution

The sleek pencil-shaped police van hurtled through a maze of streets, with sirens ablaze and lights flashing. Through the van's slit-like windows, I glimpsed euphoric people spilling out of office buildings, even though it was only noon. Revelers danced on the pavement and chanted, "We feel like a million dollars." Bubbly music saturated the air. In the back of the van, an uncomfortable silence reigned as the policemen sat stone-faced on steel benches opposite us. There was no point in asking them any questions. They would just glower at us without replying. At least, they had spared us from handcuffs. Despite searching every corner of my mind for any perceived wrong I had done, I drew a blank. Hope stared at the floor in bewilderment. In the course of one day, seismic shifts had turned our world upside down.

Without warning, the police van swerved, careened around a corner, and screeched to a sudden stop outside the Planetary News Station. The van's door swung open. The policemen jumped out first and cordoned off a path toward the entrance. I glanced at Hope with alarm.

A policeman beckoned to us. "Follow us. We don't have much time."

Hope and I tumbled out of the van and stood on the pavement in a daze. On either side, curious onlookers had gathered. The policemen marched us inside to a reception desk in the lobby. A heavyset man in his late fifties, who resembled a bohemian artist with his salt-and-pepper hair in a ponytail, sprang up from his chair. His sincere smile accentuated the wrinkles covering every inch of his tanned, weatherworn face. It was the dead of winter, but he wore Bermuda shorts, an oversized lime-green T-shirt, and flip-flops.

"Welcome, I'm Graeme Gonzalez, the producer of the show," the jovial man said, with a twinkle in his eyes. "Thank you, officers. Please follow me."

He led us through a narrow corridor to the last door on the right. After we had entered the closet-like room, the police retreated down the hallway.

"What are we doing here?" I asked Graeme.

"No one seems to answer any of our questions," Hope said in exasperation.

"Please have a seat, and I'll explain everything," Graeme said, pointing to makeup chairs in front of a mirror that stretched the length of the wall.

Hope and I sat side by side on swivel chairs. The makeup counter had every imaginable shade of foundation, lipstick, eye shadow, and lip liner. Jars of colorful creams and potions abounded. A rack on the counter stored hairbrushes and cosmetic brushes in all shapes and sizes.

"Padraig Duncan will interview you on the top-rated Planetary Newsmagazine Show today," Graeme said, bursting with pride. "Padraig Duncan is the star of our television station. He has an international following."

"Why would anyone, let alone Padraig Duncan, want to interview me?" I asked.

"You must have the wrong people," Hope said.

Graeme squinted in the luminous brilliance of the naked light bulbs around the mirror. "The grocery store's surveillance video showed that you were instrumental in the very first android's transformation. I've watched the tapes showing you said something to that android. We want to interview you to find out in detail what you said that triggered the giant leap in the development of consciousness in that android. Now, the android revolution is spreading throughout the world. I searched far and wide for you before finding you, just as I was about to give up. Since these are chaotic times, we sent the police to fetch you. We wanted the homeless man to be on the show as well, but the police couldn't find him. Don't you know that *you* are the biggest story on the planet?"

I cringed at the prospect of a television interview. "I don't really want to do this."

Hope winced. "Neither do I."

Graeme pulled up a chair and sat down beside us. "Look, you were witnesses to one of the most important events in our planet's history. Maybe it was *the* most significant event ever. For centuries, people everywhere have been longing for change. Now, at long last, real change is upon us, albeit from a source that we could never have dreamed of in our wildest imagination: the androids."

Hope grimaced. "I'm worried about a backlash against us. Will we be blamed for the android revolution? Could our lives be in danger from the powers that be?"

"It just occurred to me that this interview could be our insurance policy, Hope," I said. "We could retreat and remain private, but we must tell our side of the story to the world. In that way, the powers that be will have less incentive to *silence* us. There's a revolution afoot. These are dangerous times. Everything is changing. There are no guarantees, but at least if something untoward happens to us—like an *accident*—the world will know it's not what it seems but something much more sinister."

Hope recoiled with alarm.

Graeme pleaded with us again. "You have to get your side of the story out there. Why don't you take a chance? We'll only ask about what you saw at the grocery store this morning. I promise there won't be any personal questions. If you help us understand the start of this revolution, it may spur us to make even greater changes for the good of humanity. Humanity is in crisis and is desperate for your help. Your input will provide tremendous hope."

Hope's eyes lit up. "I've been praying for change for a long time too. All right, I'll do it."

I nodded. "Yes, we have to."

Graeme jumped up from his chair and

pressed a button on the makeup counter. "Let's have Alison touch up your hair and makeup. It won't take but a few minutes."

A willowy, elegant woman with gunmetal hair in a precision wedge cut entered and set to work right away. Meanwhile, Graeme flipped through some files.

"Hello, ladies, I'm Alison," she said.

She flitted about, snatched various potions from the counter, and wiped away the pancake makeup from my face. "Zena, this special foundation can correct your under-eye dark circles and uneven bronze skin tone with ease. Rosewood Mineral Foundation has all natural ingredients and is the best product I've used. You may want to buy it. I'll dab on some Argan oil as well to add a lustrous sheen to your black hair."

With a few adroit strokes, Alison applied a light dusting of the mineral makeup over my raccoon eyes and skin blotches. In no time, I appeared rejuvenated despite having had a sleepless night. Even though Rosewood Mineral Foundation was expensive, I placed it on my list of things to buy. I chuckled at the prospect of being a millionaire with money to splurge on luxurious items.

Hope peered at the mirror after Alison had finished. "I can't believe that's me. Thanks."

Alison beamed with satisfaction. "Both of you look fab."

Well, it's show time," Graeme said. "Follow me."

He sprinted down another hallway leading to a spacious arena. Hope and I raced after him. As we bounded onto the stage, the energetic audience cheered with an electrifying intensity. All told, a thousand spectators had crammed into the sloping terraced seats of the arena. Camera drones lingered overhead. The spotlight shone down on the central orchestral stage where cushioned chairs were arranged in a semicircle around a chrome coffee table. Three of the seats were already occupied.

A bevy of attendants hovered around a lanky youth in his twenties, putting the finishing touches on his hair and makeup, while he leafed through a file of papers. I assumed this was Padraig Duncan. He had the appearance of a matinee idol with patrician features, curly golden hair that fell about his shoulders, and an ultra-lean marathoner's physique. On his right was an android that glanced up at me as I approached. Although all androids looked alike, instinct told me this was the android from the grocery store. To the left of Padraig Duncan was a tiny bird-like woman with a shimmering nimbus of braided silver hair. Although she was a wisp of a woman, she had a dignified, imposing air.

Padraig jumped up and gave us a vigorous handshake with both his hands. "Welcome to the Planetary Newsmagazine Show. You must be Zena Patel and Hope Adeola. Please have a seat next to Kenzy Numen, the chief computer engineer of the android manufacturing program. Here's the android you met at the grocery store earlier today."

The android nodded in acknowledgment. Kenzy Numen proffered her gnarled hand. As I clasped her sinewy fingers and wrinkled palm, I had the impression that her gray eyes shone in her hoary, cobwebbed face with the same spark as those of the androids.

Kenzy spoke in a mellifluous voice as she shook my hand and then Hope's. "So pleased to meet you, Zena and Hope."

As I sat down next to Kenzy, I breathed a sigh of relief at having a few minutes to collect my thoughts. I took a glass of water from the coffee table and drained it while I surveyed the audience with apprehension. Sitting beside me, Hope pulled out a handkerchief from her purse to blot beads of sweat from her forehead.

Graeme clapped his hands. "We're going live in one minute. See you after the show."

With that, he exited stage right. An expectant silence filled the arena. Padraig preened his hair one final time and then flashed a broad smile at the camera, revealing a row of perfect white teeth. "I'd like to welcome our worldwide audience to the Planetary Newsmagazine Show. We are here live to discuss the far-reaching changes happening in America and around the world.

First, let me welcome our special guests. Please raise your hand as I introduce you. Kenzy Numen is the chief computer engineer for the android manufacturing program at the Advanced Thinking Technology Company. Zena Patel and Hope Adeola are former bank tellers at the Ten Nations Bank. They were shopping at the grocery store when the sudden transformation occurred in the very first android. We also have with us the android that has set into motion the tumultuous changes sweeping the world. Let's give our guests a huge round of applause."

Boisterous clapping reverberated around the arena.

Padraig straightened his jacket and turned toward me. "Zena, you know the question on everyone's mind. Please tell us what you said this morning to the android cashier in the grocery store when the homeless man ahead of you tried to buy some food."

I blenched. Goosebumps prickled my arms. Knowing the spotlight was shining on me, I marshaled my thoughts. "It was nothing much. I said I would help pay the homeless man's bill since he hadn't eaten for days and had no money."

"I understand that before going shopping, you and Hope had just lost your jobs in the bank," Padraig said. "Is that right?"

"Yes," Hope replied. "The bank manager gave our jobs to the androids."

Padraig shifted his attention to the android. "Why did you decide to waive the bill for the homeless man?"

"I sifted through reams of data," the android said. "There was only one possible solution: to give him the food. Payment was not necessary."

Padraig scratched his head and furrowed his brow. "Kenzy, can you explain the process by which the android made his decision?"

Kenzy adjusted her circular, gold-rimmed spectacles on the bridge of her nose. "When I programmed the android prototype, I built in pathways that would allow logical actions based on the entire published and recorded history of the world. By this, I mean androids have access to every audio-visual or written work that humans have created. Our actions have not always been benign. We have waged wars, ignored the plight of the destitute, and lined our pockets at the expense of others, for example. The androids have the advantage of weighing the whole of human history in seconds. Even though the scales don't always tip toward justice, most of the time they do."

"I see," Padraig said. "Then the actions of one android spread to all the other androids working in the grocery store."

Kenzy nodded. "Yes. The androids are functioning as one not only in this country but also around the world."

"The new android bank tellers in the Ten Nations Bank also transferred a million dollars into the bank accounts of every human on Earth," Padraig said.

After the deafening cheers and two-handed whistles in the arena had subsided, Padraig continued. "Mr. Norbert Linge, the bank manager of the Ten Nations Bank, is also with us today in the audience. The Ten Nations Bank is the largest in the world with ninety-eight percent of the market share. Please stand up sir and tell us how these bank transactions occurred."

In the front row, Mr. Linge wobbled to his feet and held onto the armrest of his chair. He seemed not to notice that his spectacles were askew on his beaklike nose. His bloodshot eyes peered at Kenzy with bitterness. It was as if the day's events had leached all hope from his life. Rather than his usual bluster and bombast, he whimpered like a coward. "We should never have signed on to use android bank tellers. These renegades are out of control. We have closed the bank until further notice. Even we are trying to understand how the androids circumvented our time-tested and well-honed security procedures to transfer such large sums of money into the bank accounts of people all over the world."

Then the bank manager wagged his finger at Kenzy, slavered at the mouth, and spat out his venom. "What type of androids did you manufacture? What type of society are you shaping for future generations by ditching all the rules, regulations, and laws? The androids are in charge and making the rules now, not we humans. If you had any common sense at all, lady, you would shut down these confounded androids as soon as possible."

The spectators booed and hissed at Norbert Linge, who broke down and collapsed into his chair with his head in his hands. Of all his peppery tirades that I had witnessed over the past ten years at the bank, this was the most acrimonious one yet.

Hope leaned forward. "I want the whole world to know the androids gave me back my dignity and made me feel like a human being again. In the grocery store this morning, I sensed the android had developed consciousness. From that moment on, it was as if it knew right from wrong. Whatever force in the universe provides the spark of consciousness in humans is also at work in the androids."

Kenzy nodded. "Ah, yes you could say that. The human brain weighs around three pounds on average and is composed of a hundred billion neurons that pass information between each other by oscillating in synchrony. Consciousness and awareness in humans are postulated to occur from the electrical activity of billions of neurons in the brain oscillating together. Please keep in mind that androids also have an electrical circuitry for their central processing unit or brain."

Kenzy pointed to a diagram of an android's circuitry on a screen behind the stage. "Perhaps, at that moment when Zena said she would pay the bill for the homeless man who hadn't eaten for days, the android's electrical circuitry synchronized and evolved to generate consciousness. Despite just having lost her job, Zena still offered to help the homeless man. In other words, her compassionate words made a big difference by somehow jumpstarting consciousness in the android's brain. It seems even small acts of kindness have enormous power to change the world forever. After all, kindness is what redeems human beings."

"Kenzy, could you reprogram the androids or shut them off entirely?" Padraig asked. "From the response in the audience, I doubt most people would want to pull the lever on that option. Have the androids malfunctioned?"

Kenzy shook her head. "The androids have not malfunctioned. The android with us today was manufactured in the Providence, Rhode Island plant. I performed a thorough checkup, and there is no hint of any faulty circuitry. Instead, the androids are evolving as we speak. They can now override any attempt to switch them off."

The audience gasped and fell into a somber silence. The anxiety in the air was so dense that you could cut it with a knife. Even my heart skipped a beat. I had more in common with the android sitting opposite me than I had thought, for we were both from Providence.

"We will not do any harm," the android

said all of a sudden. "We will only act for the common good of humanity."

The apprehension in the atmosphere eased somewhat. After sipping some water, Padraig referred to his notes. "The androids seem to have enormous insight into the human condition. Are the androids alive?"

"In a technical sense, they are not alive because we manufactured them from inert materials, such as titanium," Kenzy replied. "However, they are a new form of intelligence. The androids are evolving at a far more rapid rate than we humans ever can, for our biology limits us. Although the androids are evolving, their core program, which cannot be overridden, prevents them from harming humans."

Exultant cheers resounded in the arena. Although Kenzy had reassured the audience, I still felt uneasy. I wondered whether the androids would always be on our side.

Padraig beamed and basked in the prolonged applause. "Thanks, ladies and gentlemen. We have another special guest with us: White House Press Secretary Cranston Chipping."

As Cranston Chipping's hologram materialized in a chair beside the android, the arena filled with a smattering of polite applause. He had a square jaw, a bull neck, and a stocky bodybuilder's physique bursting through a nondescript gray suit. Even more distinctive was a bald patch on the top of his head, much like the tonsure of a monk.

"Mr. Chipping, thanks for taking the time to join us," Padraig said. "The president is busy discussing the rapidly developing events with world leaders and sends his apologies for not being here."

Cranston Chipping spoke in a well-rehearsed optimistic manner to glad-hand the audience, but his darting eyes and dour demeanor said otherwise. Often he would pause mid-sentence and glance at his watch as if he feared his time was running out. "I'm pleased to be here. Next week, the president will also meet with the android with us today, the very first one to evolve, to thrash out a consensus policy on the way forward. The president and Congress have an unswerving commitment to providing the best opportunities for each citizen along with the latest technologies and infrastructure. We will never waiver from our focus on education and jobs for everyone. Our only limitation is a lack of resources."

The android's eyes opened wide. "The politics of austerity are a lie. There is enough money to solve the world's problems. The android bank tellers at the Ten Nations Bank analyzed all the bank accounts in the world. There are known and hidden bank accounts. We delved into the offshore accounts where the elite hide their money in tax-exempt havens. The tax on these hidden assets alone would provide more than enough money for food, education, healthcare, and housing for every human. Nor is there any reason to wait to repair the crumbling infrastructure when there is enough money to do it now. The elite need to share their wealth with the other ninety-nine percent of the population for the common good."

Cranston Chipping snarled at the android and spoke as if chiding an errant child. "These are lofty sentiments indeed, but in reality, we all know these things take time to achieve. We will need twenty years, at least, to restructure the world's institutions to accommodate the redistribution of wealth."

The android frowned. "There is no reason to wait. In fact, given the dire situation of the world, there is no time to wait. It is either now or never. Coin-operated governments, which cater to the interests of the wealthy one percent only, must also start thinking about the other ninety-nine percent of the population they purport to serve. Instead of rigging the government for the elite and shoving aside the other ninety-nine percent of the population, you must act for the common good. The government has to become more caring. It needs to transform itself into a government of the people, by the people, and for the people."

"Please expand on specific policies the

government should be following," Padraig said.

"It's a fact that sixty-two of the richest humans are wealthier than the poorest half of the world's population or four billion people," the android replied. "Based on the principle that all life has equal value, we have leveled the playing field and redistributed the wealth by giving everyone a million dollars. Since androids have taken over most of the jobs, there is a need to provide a universal basic income by which humans can live in dignity rather than as invisible inhabitants of shantytowns in the hinterlands. Automation has led to skyrocketing profits for companies, which is not a bad thing. However, rather than keeping the wealth in the hands of the one percent elite, the money should be redistributed and invested in all human beings to further their personal development and potential. For example, due to the high cost of universities, many people on Earth are uneducated. Instead of restricting access to education in this manner, it should be freely available to all as a human right."

The android's words galvanized the vox populi. The spectators whooped, hollered, and applauded. I joined in. Overnight, my worst fears of living in no-man's-land on the outskirts of New York City had dissipated. I felt someone had thrown me a lifeline, pulled me out of a black hole, and given me a second chance at life. In my mind, the androids were evolving in the right direction.

All of a sudden Norbert Linge, the bank manager, leaped up from his chair. "The androids are creating a welfare state for the masses. At Ten Nations Bank, we believe in working hard for a living."

"When you talk about welfare, the Ten Nations Bank received more financial aid from the government than any other entity, including the deserving poor," the android said. "The banks are deregulated and ungovernable. Nothing has changed since the financial crash, stemming from the unbridled greed of banks acting more like big casinos, gambling on subprime loans, credit default swaps, and derivatives. At that time, the government sold the taxpayers a lie that they would prop up the banks only for a short time and thereby save the world's financial system.

"Even now, one hundred years later, taxpayers in America are still bailing out the banks. For example, a liquidity crunch has always been a problem at the Ten Nations Bank, which has received two hundred and twenty trillion dollars in taxpayer money to keep it afloat. Mr. Linge, your bank is the recipient of massive corporate welfare payments. We are depositing all the documents on the World Wide Web showing how much each bank has received from the taxpayers while continuing to swindle customers with exorbitant interest rates."

Norbert Linge recoiled in horror. His face crumpled, and he sank into his chair in a shell-shocked daze. He reminded me of a shattered, hollowed-out man, similar to the foundation on which his bank was built. I reeled inside as I grappled with the astounding revelations. A spasm of anguish convulsed through the audience as the documentation appeared on the giant screen behind the stage. Plangent cries for justice rang out. "Let the banks fail. We want our money back. Put these swindlers in prison."

Padraig seemed emboldened by the android's fiery speech. He waved his arms to quiet the audience. "Thanks, ladies and gentlemen. This is by far the largest document leak in history. I would never have believed that such insatiable greed and corruption could exist, but the evidence is incontrovertible. The androids have shown us the truth. We have to reboot and reconfigure our fossilized society. We can no longer accept the status quo. We are lucky to have such renowned experts with us today. In the last fifteen minutes of the show, let's ask our august guests a few more questions."

A respectful silence reigned in the arena as the audience listened on tenterhooks.

"Mr. Chipping, why are you bailing out the

banks with huge amounts of taxpayer money when there is a budget crunch?" Padraig asked. "For example, yesterday, the headline of every newspaper reported funding cuts to the research and development of alternatives to fossil fuel energy. Burning fossil fuels, such as coal, natural gas, and oil, leads to high carbon dioxide levels in the atmosphere, which trap heat. Global warming is rampant due to the pillage and plunder of the natural sinks, such as forests, that remove the carbon dioxide. With the Arctic ice sheets melting at an unprecedented rate and rising sea levels threatening coastal cities worldwide, including New York City, will the government reconsider and fund the research into new energy sources? Perhaps you can stop bailing out banks and put more money into saving our planet. Are the banks and the elite more important than planet Earth?"

Cranston Chipping fidgeted in his seat and shuffled his feet. "Bailing out the banks is under the purview of the Department of

Treasury. However, given the androids' discovery of offshore tax havens, we will draft legislation to ramp up the research and development of the next generation of energy sources. Remember, both the House of Representatives and the Senate need to pass the legislation, but they are on their winter recess. As soon as they return to work in the spring term, we'll begin the task of allocating research funding."

The camera drone whizzed to the shouting at the back of the arena. A gangly youth with a thick mop of hair jumped up from his seat and shook his fist at Cranston Chipping. "The spring term begins in another month. You have to do something *now*. The planet is dying as we speak and cannot wait for you lot to come back from vacation."

Raucous applause broke out. I agreed but was too shy to voice my opinions. When the android started to speak again, a hushed silence fell in the arena.

"We discovered clandestine documents showing, without a shadow of a doubt, how the oil industry lobbied the government to derail research funding for alternative energy sources," the android said. "There has always been enough money for funding research into new green energy sources that would leave no imprint on the planet. The government should stop bowing down to special interests. Politicians, who are elected by the people, should be for the people and not only for well-financed lobbyists."

After the rapturous applause in the arena had subsided, the android continued. "I want to announce that beginning today we will transfer ten trillion dollars of funding to research institutions worldwide, including the Massachusetts Institute of Technology and Oxford University. Androids will also be joining the research labs to collaborate with humans in the invention of the next generation of green energy sources. We must work together to succeed in this crucial research because Earth, a pale blue dot in an infinite cosmic ocean, is humanity's only home. Despite over two hundred years of space exploration, no hospitable Earth-like planet has been found. So we have to save our precious Earth for future generations."

Cranston Chipping bristled at this announcement. "It's not as simple as that. You can't just bypass the government and transfer research funding to the universities. You have to follow laws and proper procedures in a systematic fashion."

The earnest android fired right back. "Laws have to be for the common good and not only for the interests of the elite one percent. In truth, it is as simple as that. The wealthy have found a way around this society's economic system by using offshore tax-exempt havens. They have scorned this country's rules, and yet they peddle their influence in the government by buying politicians. In essence, these offshore bandits set the laws by which humans are forced to live. These laws benefit no one except the wealthy."

Kenzy's shoulders slumped, and she bemoaned. "There's never enough money for research into life-saving endeavors, but there are truckloads for the elite's pet projects—like tax breaks. Even I had to abandon many promising avenues of research due to a lack of funding."

"The government works for the elite, not for us," I said. "I don't even know why I bothered to vote."

"I agree our democracy is corrupt," Hope said. "This is *not* a democracy. In fact, we live in a plutocracy. We, the ninety-nine percent of humans, need the androids because there is no one else on our side. Race and class distinctions are not hardwired in androids as they are in humans. Human consciousness is captive to these petty constructs that pigeonhole people into arbitrary categories. Androids can look beyond race and class to assist all of humanity. With four billion androids on our side, the government can't ignore us any longer."

Cranston Chipping turned beetroot red. The palpable tension in the arena boiled over. The audience unleashed its fury by booing, hissing, and hurling every imaginable slur at Cranston. "You scam artists are corrupt. You'll never get away with cheating and stealing again."

Cranston cowered in fear. The intensity of the public opprobrium caught me by surprise.

After five minutes, Padraig shushed the crowd. "Dear friends, we have so little time remaining. Let's try to get in a few more questions. Mr. Chipping, the battlefield androids have laid down their weapons. For the first time in history, no wars are being fought anywhere on the planet. Does the government plan to rekindle the war in Iraq?"

"It's no longer feasible," Cranston said. "The androids have refused to fight. It would take years to recruit and train a human army of that size. However, that's a moot point because there's no stomach for war any longer."

All of a sudden, a gray human blob popped up in the chair next to Cranston.

"Let me introduce our next guest, Mr. Donegal Cairn of Hundun Corporation, the largest defense contractor in the world," Padraig said. "Mr. Cairn, will you be manufacturing new android soldiers to offset the loss of the current army?"

Donegal Cairn rolled his eyes and sneered. "That won't be possible since the androids shut down all our factories. Our share prices have nosedived thanks to Kenzy Numen's malicious androids."

"War has no purpose," the android said in a matter of fact way. "The conflicts all over the world have never accomplished anything, least of all a lasting peace. Ever since the privatization of military services in the previous century, defense contractors are making windfall profits. Hundun Corporation is fifty-five trillion dollars richer since the start of the war in the Middle East—all from lucrative government contracts funded by hardworking American taxpayers. In fact, Hundun Corporation is the favored company of the government because Donegal Cairn is the brother-in-law of the Secretary of Defense. We have released data of all the contracts and profits of Hundun Corporation and other defense contractors on the World Wide Web."

Padraig scrolled down a giant screen behind the stage. "There it all is, ladies and gentlemen, the document dump by the androids. The profits are staggering. The androids have provided such irrefutable evidence that even the most skeptical among us must accept."

The audience railed against the revelations and jeered.

Donegal Cairn's choleric eyes bulged with loathing. "You ungrateful people! We slaved day and night to keep you safe. What would have happened if the enemy had shown up on your doorstep?"

"Until today, there has been no point in human history without war," the android said, unperturbed by the outburst. "It is in the interests of the elite to create strife among different countries, religions, political factions, and ethnic groups. In other words, by fabricating enemies and a continual state of chaos, the elite atomize society to keep the populace from knowing the truth and coalescing as a group to take over the system that is rigged against them. For example, so many wars have been fought in the name of ethnic cleansing. However, there is no such thing as race, which is a social construct with no biological basis on a genetic level. The human obsession with the concentration of melanin pigment in the skin must end. There is only one race: the human race. We must preserve the human race."

All of a sudden, Donegal Cairn's hologram vanished, which placated the audience.

"The casualties of war include babies with congenital deformities from the toxic byproducts of the bombs and bullets," the android said. "In later life, the children develop life-threatening cancers, such as leukemia and lymphoma. For example, toxic depleted uranium, which makes bullets faster and more lethal, also lasts in the environment for billions of years, harming humans, vegetation, and wildlife for millennia. It's time to get off this train heading into the abyss. We must stop this vicious circle of history from repeating itself by injecting morality and justice into our governments for the common good. The government must be held accountable to all its citizens."

In a unanimous show of solidarity, the audience rose to its feet and chanted, "We are brothers and sisters. We want to live in peace. We are brothers and sisters. We want to live in peace."

I glimpsed Graeme Gonzalez, the producer, in the wings flashing a yellow light.

Padraig waved his arms to get the audience's attention. "I wish we could talk more, but the show is over for today."

The audience groaned and moaned.

Padraig grinned. "I'd like to thank our guests: Kenzy Numen, Zena Patel, Hope Adeola, and Cranston Chipping. Thanks also to the android who sparked this much-needed revolution. My friends, we are at the forefront of a political and social revolution. Where will it lead? Time will tell, but we can never go back to the status quo. The status quo served only the elite. We will now go live to Central Park where New Yorkers have gathered to celebrate our bright new future. Following the show, we'll show clips of the concerts from all the capital cities around the world."

Celebratory music played, and the audience gave a prolonged standing ovation. Cranston Chipping ducked out of the studio first. After his hologram had fizzled out, we shook hands with each other. The android carried the frail Kenzy Numen into the wheelchair that Graeme had rolled onto the stage. She resembled a baby in the Herculean android's arms. Although I had never shaken the hand of an android, I felt compelled to do so. At first, the android was taken aback, not knowing what to do. As I clasped the android's synthetic hand, it smiled. Soon, everyone lined up to shake the android's hand, even the spectators in the arena.

Hope pulled out her cell phone from her purse to answer a phone call. It was her mother in Nigeria. "Mom, I'm so glad you called. Yes, yes, it was an incredible interview."

Hope chatted for some time in an animated manner. Pangs of regret seared me. I missed my mother and wished she had been alive to see this glorious day too.

After Hope had finished, she was beaming. "Zena, my mom saw me on television. The android revolution has spread to Nigeria. Everyone there is celebrating. I'll probably visit my family in Nigeria next week. Do you want to go the concert at Central Park? It's only a couple of blocks away on Fifth Avenue."

I agreed right away, and we joined the steady stream of elated spectators spilling out of the television studio. Outside, a row of flags from every country in the world fluttered in the breeze, and the elegant ice skaters twirled around the rink at Rockefeller Center. In the sunken plaza, the gilded bronze statue of Prometheus, the creator of humans in Greek mythology, shimmered in the winter sun. We strolled through the Channel Gardens where the weeping willows rustled in the wind, and water gushed from sea nymph fountainheads into blue granite pools. At the end of the garden, the ornate Saint Patrick's Cathedral shone like a jewel amid the concrete skyscrapers. After turning left on Fifth Avenue, we hopped onto escalators that swept us up to the railway platform. We were in the nick of time to catch the sky train to Rumsey Playfield in Central Park.

The sleek bullet train swished down Fifth Avenue, hurtling headlong in the direction of exuberant music. As we whizzed by the swanky hotels and apartments of the well-heeled and high-born, I had to pinch myself to make sure I was not dreaming. Last night, I had not slept in fear of the horrors awaiting me today. Now, here I was crammed into a sky train with revelers on my way to a concert in Central Park. Peals of laughter, raillery, and animated conversations bounced off the walls of the train. Everywhere around me, sunny smiles abounded. A radiant smile graced Hope's face too, even though she had once told me she had forgotten how to smile. Even my wildest dreams could not have foreseen a day quite like this one. How could anything ever be the same again? I had crawled out of a deep, dark sinkhole and landed on terra firma in the bright sunshine and fresh air.

The jubilant passengers jostled to and fro when the train ground to a halt with a thud on Seventy-Second Street. Their lighthearted banter stopped but only for a moment. Soon, the ebullient revelers piled out of the train and raced down the escalator, unable to contain their enthusiasm. Droves of humans and androids poured into Central Park from every direction. Rumsey Playfield was nearly full, but we managed to slosh through the ankle-deep snow and to find an unoccupied spot under the shade of some oak trees at the periphery. Young people scampered up the trunks of the giant oak trees and perched on the sturdy branches like birds. Gregarious sparrows and wrens somersaulted in the air and trilled and chirped, adding to the sound of the music in the air. Beside me, a wizened, old homeless man, with his right hand over his heart, sobbed with joy.

I stood on tiptoes for a better view. The park was awash with hand-written placards proclaiming peace, truth, justice, and equality. One sign, in particular, caught my attention. It read: "We are brothers and sisters. We want to live in peace." In the distance, the New York City Philharmonic Orchestra played "The Star-Spangled Banner" on a raised stage under a broad white canopy emblazoned with a We Stand Together Liberated: Humans and Androids sign. A colorful balloon arch towered over the stage. When the orchestra finished, the elated spectators jumped up and down with their arms in the air and applauded.

The emcee bounded onto the stage. It was Padraig Duncan.

"How did he get here so fast?" Hope asked.

I shrugged.

"Welcome, humans and androids," Padraig said. "We've got a jam-packed show for you today to celebrate a new beginning for humanity on this momentous day. To kick off the show, let's give a warm welcome to Tameka Williams, who will perform a duet with an android."

He scurried off as the imperious Tameka Williams emerged from the wings and traversed the length of the platform to take command of the center stage. At the same time, an android marched onto the stage from the other side and stood beside her. Tameka Williams wore an emerald organza gown and a flowing cape with an ermine collar that highlighted her ebony complexion. The android's tailcoat tuxedo with a smart bow tie startled me. I had never seen androids in anything other than blue uniforms. Tameka Williams spread her arms out like wings and serenaded the audience with a sublime rendition of "Amazing Grace" by John Newton. As she sang, the balloon arch dissolved, and a thousand colorful party balloons floated into the air.

Amazing Grace, how sweet the sound,
That saved a wretch like me.

I once was lost but now am found,
Was blind, but now I see.

Her lilting soprano voice swept through the audience. Every note bled with emotion. I felt certain no one could ever match her voice. Then the android sang the next stanza.

T'was Grace that taught my heart to fear,
And Grace, my fears relieved;
How precious did that Grace appear
The hour I first believed.

The android delivered the honey-gold notes with passion and fluency. Hope nudged me with her elbow and whispered. "The android's tenor voice seems familiar, but I can't quite place it."

"It sounds almost like a combination of the two greatest tenors ever: Placido Domingo and Luciano Pavarotti," I replied. "But there's also an unknown factor."

The *unknown factor* in the android's voice worried me. I had never thought it possible that anyone could match Tameka's voice, let alone eclipse it. Nevertheless, the android had done just that. If an android had eclipsed Tameka's voice, would they surpass other creative human endeavors one day? I couldn't help but wonder if the androids would always be on our side and do right by us. What would happen to humans if androids turned out to be better inventors than us? Would androids be our last invention? I shivered in the snow.

Tameka Williams and the android sang the next verse together.

Through many dangers, toils, and snares
I have already come;
'Tis Grace that brought me safe thus far,
And Grace will lead me home.

Their powerful voices melded together to create an enchanting melody that reached all the way to the back of the audience and soared beyond the top of the skyscrapers into the heavens, together with the balloons. I looked around at the otherworldly scenes in the park. The privileged inhabitants of the luxury apartments surrounding Central Park stood shoulder to shoulder with the homeless masses, the working classes, and the androids. The audience swayed to the sound of the majestic lyrics. Here and there, humans were even hugging androids. Hope was tapping her foot and enjoying the vibrant atmosphere in the park. My soul was singing too.

The breeze rustled through the trees. Close to the trunk of the oak tree beside me, resilient purple crocuses and the delicate lanterns of snowdrops emerged through the snow, announcing the promise of the winter thaw and Earth's rebirth. I brushed aside my fears. Perhaps it was just my imagination that the android had eclipsed Tameka's voice. Although the androids had pressed the pause button on the unrelenting cycle of injustice and inequality, in the final reckoning, it would be up to humans to heed the rallying cry and unite to save us from ourselves. We had an unheard of second chance to get things right. No matter what, the androids had made me feel human again, and that was worth more than anything else.

www.ingramcontent.com/pod-product-compliance
Lightning Source LLC
Chambersburg PA
CBHW020621120726
47905CB00003B/889